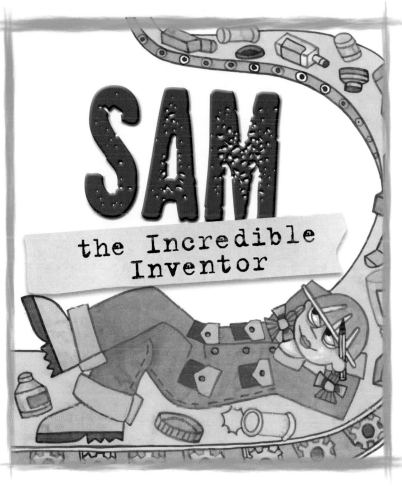

# SAM
## the Incredible Inventor

Lee Aucoin, *Creative Director*
Jamey Acosta, *Senior Editor*
Heidi Fiedler, *Editor*
Produced and designed by
Denise Ryan & Associates
Illustration © Jane Wallace-Mitchell
Rachelle Cracchiolo, *Publisher*

**Teacher Created Materials**
5301 Oceanus Drive
Huntington Beach, CA 92649-1030
http://www.tcmpub.com
**Paperback: ISBN: 978-1-4333-5610-0**
**Library Binding: ISBN: 978-1-4807-1732-9**
© 2014 Teacher Created Materials

Written by
Alan Trussell-Cullen

Illustrated by
Jane Wallace-Mitchell

# Contents

**Chapter One**

Sam the Incredible Inventor . . . . . .3

**Chapter Two**

Sam Makes a Splash . . . . . . . . . .11

**Chapter Three**

Sam Gets to Work . . . . . . . . . . .19

**Chapter Four**

Luigi's Grand Opening . . . . . . .27

## Chapter One

# SAM

the Incredible Inventor

Sam loves inventing things and, unlike most kids, she likes doing chores. Well, that's because she invents machines to do the chores for her!

One of Sam's newest inventions is the Trash Taking Out Machine. She has to take out the trash once a week. That's a chore she really doesn't like, so she decided to invent a machine to do it for her. It looks like this.

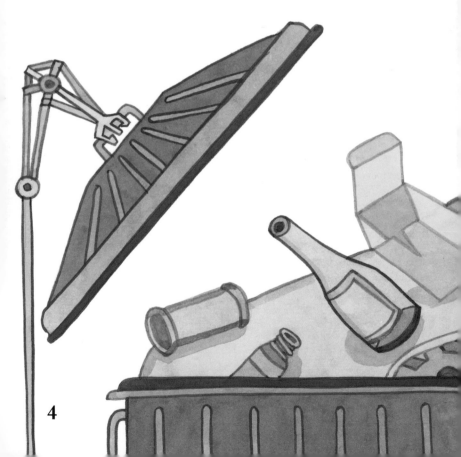

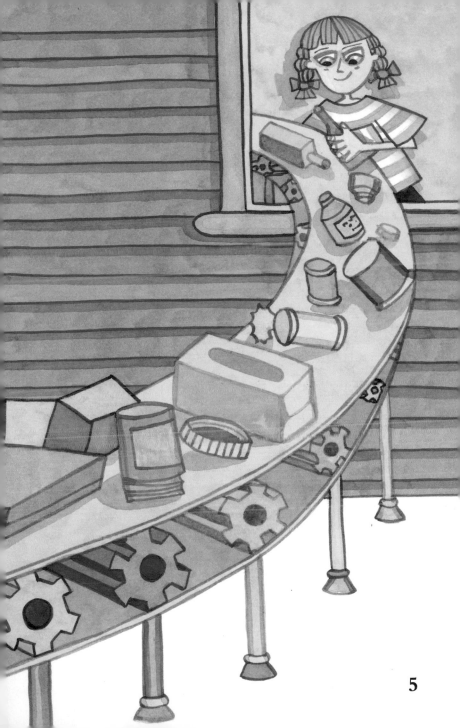

Sam has invented a lot of other things, too. She used to have trouble eating spaghetti—but not anymore. She invented a Super Spaghetti Twirling Machine to help her eat it. All she has to do is hit a switch and open her mouth.

Sam also hates dusting, so she invented a Do It All Dusting Machine. A special ceiling fan swirls long feathers around the room. It makes people sneeze, but it does get rid of dust.

7

Sam loves her bike and all the extras she invented for it, like her Barking Bell. She is also very proud of her Rain Activated Umbrella. One drop of rain, and it opens automatically. She says it's one of her best inventions ever.

But even the best inventions can have unexpected results. That's what Sam learned one wet day.

## Chapter Two

# SAM

## Makes a Splash

On this particular day, Sam was riding home from soccer practice. It was a sunny day without a cloud in the sky. Sam was scheming. Maybe she could invent a Super Smart Goalkeeper to help her play.

But suddenly, Sam was drenched in water! Of course, her Rain Activated Umbrella opened immediately, but then Sam couldn't see where she was going. She rode off the street, across the sidewalk, and right into the middle of a construction site!

That was when she realized where all the water was coming from. A bulldozer had broken a pipe. Everyone was running around trying to turn it off, but nothing seemed to be working.

Sam jumped off her bike, grabbed her soccer ball, and shoved it in the broken pipe. Finally, the water stopped. Without even trying, Sam had invented the Soccer Ball Water Plug!

Mr. Hegel, the man in charge, came running up to Sam. He had a big smile on his face.

"Thank you! That was really clever!" he said. "And your bike looks amazing, too! I've never seen one like that. Did you make it?"

Sam blushed. "Oh, I just like inventing things," she said.

"I can see that," said Mr. Hegel. Say, how would you like to do a bit of inventing for us? We have to get Luigi's new restaurant finished in time for the grand opening on Saturday. He'll be mad if we don't finish in time, and we still have so much to do!

Wow! Sam had never used her inventions to help someone else before.

"I'd love to help," said Sam. "What needs to be done?"

"I have a list of things to do," said Mr. Hegel, and he handed it to Sam.

1. Finish putting tiles on the roof.

2. Nail down the floorboards.

3. Paint all the walls and ceilings.

4. Set up a new kitchen for Luigi.

"I can help you! Let me think for a while, and I'll see what I can invent. Maybe we can make the work easier," Sam said. As she biked home, her head was spinning with ideas. This was going to be her biggest project ever. But could they really finish the building in just four days?

## Chapter Three

# SAM
### Gets to Work

The next day was Tuesday. Sam was at the construction site first thing in the morning.

"It's a great day for roof tiling!" she announced as she dragged in her Precision Roof Tiling Cannon. She loaded it up with tiles for the roof. "Ready! Aim! Fire!" Sam yelled.

Immediately, the machine started shooting tiles onto the roof. Each tile was sticky with glue and landed exactly where it was supposed to be stuck. Twenty minutes later, the roof was finished.

"That's amazing!" said Mr. Hegel. "But what about the floorboards?"

"Tomorrow," Sam replied.

On Wednesday, Sam arrived with her Bam Bam Hammer. It could hammer fifty nails all at the same time. Sam turned on her machine. *Bam! Bam! Bam!* In minutes, the job was done.

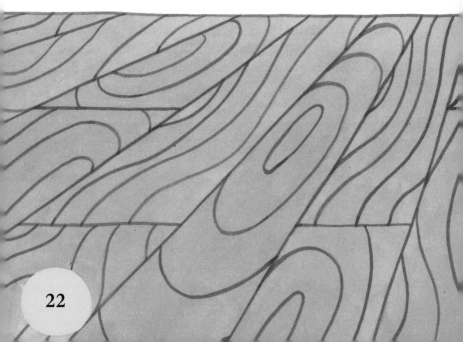

When Sam arrived on Thursday, Mr. Hegel was panicking. "How are you going to paint all the walls and the ceiling in one day?"

"No problem!" said Sam. She pushed in her new Roll-On Paint Machine. The paint was stored on big rolls of sticky tape. In a matter of minutes, Sam and the workers unrolled the tape and stuck it to the walls and the ceiling.

"There you are, Mr. Hegel. The job is done!" Sam announced. The restaurant was looking better every day.

## Chapter Four

# Luigi's
## Grand Opening

On Friday, Luigi came in to see how the work was going. "Where is my kitchen?" he shouted. "How am I supposed to make wonderful Italian dishes tomorrow without a kitchen?"

"No problem!" said Sam as she and the workers dragged in a strange-looking machine.

"Holy macaroni! What is that?" yelled Luigi.

"This is my Everything Kitchen Cooker," said Sam.

"But what does it do?" asked Luigi.

"Everything!" said Sam. "It bakes, fries, toasts, steams, microwaves, whips, mixes, chills, and freezes!"

"Magnificent!" declared Luigi. "I can't wait to try it!"

Soon, Luigi had everything working. "Thank you, Sam!" he said. "Come to the grand opening tomorrow and bring your family. You're all welcome here!"

On Saturday, everyone came to Luigi's grand opening. Luigi had kept the best table for Sam and her family. And what do you think Sam had for lunch? Spaghetti, of course! She ate it with one of her very own Super Spaghetti Twirlers.

"Here's to Sam, the amazing inventor!" Luigi said. Everyone cheered!

**Alan Trussell-Cullen** lives in Auckland, New Zealand. Alan writes children's books, screenplays, plays, and television shows. He has worked with teachers throughout the United States, as well as in Sweden, Australia, and the United Kingdom. Alan also wrote *The Lonely Penguin's Blog* for Read! Explore! Imagine! Fiction Readers.

**Jane Wallace-Mitchell** lives in Melbourne, Australia. Jane trained as a graphic designer, but has worked mostly as a children's book illustrator. She is also a very talented potter and crafter. Jane's detailed and brightly colored work can be seen in the Read! Explore! Imagine! Fiction Readers *How to Be a Kitten, Safari Camp,* and *Space Ace.*